# Batty Betty's Spells

To Phoebe H and Amelia

First published 2004
Evans Brothers Limited
2A Portman Mansions
Chiltern St
London W1U 6NR

British Library Cataloguing in Publication Data

Robinson, Hilary, 1962-
Batty Betty's spells. - (Zig zags)
1. Magic - Juvenile fiction. 2. Children's Stories
I. Title
823. 9'14 [J]

ISBN 0237526697

Printed in China by WKT Company Limited

Series Editor: Louise John
Design: Robert Walster
Production: Jenny Mulvanny
Series Consultant: Gill Matthews

# ZIG ZAG

# Batty Betty's Spells

by Hilary Robinson
illustrated by Belinda Worsley

# Batty Betty always found…

...she got her spells
mixed up.

So when she tried to mend
a plate, it turned into a...

# cup!

Her very worst day of all
was when she blocked
the sink.

She cast a spell to sort it
out and turned her black
cat…

Things did not get better
when she started
a spring clean.

15

The spell for this
went very wrong and
turned her pink cat...

Ah, she thought, I know a spell to make my messy bed.

But when she waved
her magic wand,
it turned her green cat...

# red!

Betty mixed a magic spell to clean her bathroom pipes.

23

But oh dear me – her poor red cat was...

# head to foot in
## stripes!

ha

ha

25

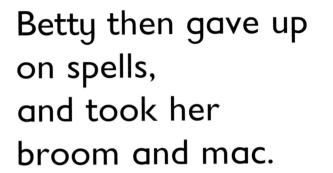

Betty then gave up
on spells,
and took her
broom and mac.

She flies around the sky
at night…

... so her striped cat looks

# black!

Why not try reading another ZigZag book?

**Dinosaur Planet**      ISBN: 0 237 52667 0
by David Orme and Fabiano Fiorin

**Tall Tilly**      ISBN: 0 237 52668 9
by Jillian Powell and Tim Archbold

**Batty Betty's Spells**   ISBN: 0 237 52669 7
by Hilary Robinson and Belinda Worsley

**The Thirsty Moose**    ISBN: 0 237 52666 2
by David Orme and Mike Gordon

**The Clumsy Cow**    ISBN: 0 237 52656 5
by Julia Moffatt and Lisa Williams

**Open Wide!**      ISBN: 0 237 52657 3
by Julia Moffatt and Anni Axworthy